THE UGLY DUMPLING

MINNEAPOLIS, MINNESOTA

THE UGLY DUMPLING

a story by
STEPHANIE CAMPISI

illustrated by
SHAHAR KOBER

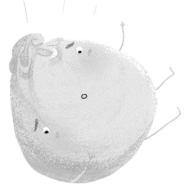

Published by Mighty Media Kids, an imprint of
Mighty Media Press, a division of Mighty Media, Inc.

Library of Congress Cataloging-in-Publication Data

Names: Campisi, Stephanie, author. | Kober, Shahar, illustrator.
Title: The ugly dumpling / Stephanie Campisi ; illustrated by Shahar Kober.
Description: Minneapolis, MN : Mighty Media Kids, [2016] | 2015 | Summary:
 An ugly dumpling is ignored and sad until an encouraging cockroach sees
 the dumpling's inner beauty and helps it discover its true identity and
 realize being different is beautiful after all.
Identifiers: LCCN 2015040899| ISBN 9781938063671 (hardback) | ISBN
 9781938063695 (ebook)
Subjects: | CYAC: Self-esteem--Fiction. | Friendship--Fiction. | BISAC:
 JUVENILE FICTION / Social Issues / Self-Esteem & Self-Reliance. | JUVENILE
 FICTION / Fairy Tales & Folklore / Adaptations. | JUVENILE FICTION /
 Social Issues / Friendship. | JUVENILE FICTION / Cooking & Food.
Classification: LCC PZ7.1.C35 Ug 2016 | DDC [E]--dc23
LC record available at http://lccn.loc.gov/2015040899

Art direction, book design, and hand lettering by Christa Schneider,
Mighty Media, Inc.

Printed and manufactured in the United States
North Mankato, Minnesota

Distributed by Publishers Group West

First edition

10 9 8 7 6 5 4 3 2 1

Stephanie Campisi
is an Australian-born, Portland-based author
and dumpling aficionado. She has combined
her passion for food and love of wordplay into
her debut picture book.

Shahar Kober
is an award-winning illustrator of over thirty
children's books. His work has been published
in the USA and around the world. Shahar
lives in a small town in northern Israel with his
wife, two boys, a dog, and a cat. He teaches
illustration for animation in Israel.

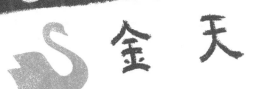

鵝 酒 家

Dedication

To Granddad,

who always loved

a good yarn.

Once upon a time,
perhaps last week,
or even last night,
at your local dim sum restaurant...

there was an UGLY DUMPLING.

But all dumplings are ugly, you say!

Which is a very good point.

But this was not just **any** ugly dumpling.

Like **this** one.

Or **that** one.

Or that one on the **floor.**

This
ugly dumpling
was ugly
in its
OWN
ugly way.

No matter what it did—

wrinkling its brow,

standing up tall,

wearing pleated pants—

it was in a lonely
only category

of ONE.

Uneaten and ignored.

Until,

along came a cockroach.

There was silence.

Except for the [of the wok]

and the **THWACK** of the cleaver

and the **WHOOSH** of the cockroach's heart swelling with love.

But the ugly dumpling noticed none of this.

The cockroach wept for the ugly dumpling.

Then it reached out an arm.
(Or a leg.)

"I will show you the beauty of the world,"

it said.

And it
DID.

The ugly dumpling was on top of the world.

The beautiful, beautiful world.

But then,

the ugly dumpling saw something:

another ugly dumpling.

The ugly dumpling was
not an ugly dumpling.
It was not a dumpling
at ALL.

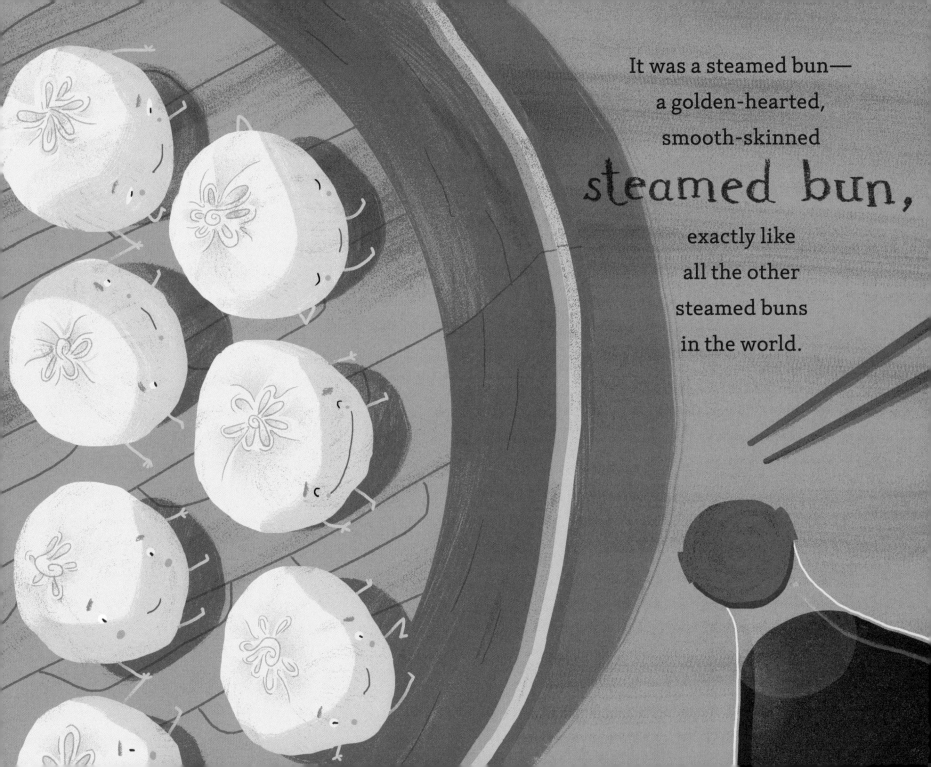

It was a steamed bun—
a golden-hearted,
smooth-skinned
steamed bun,
exactly like
all the other
steamed buns
in the world.

The ugly dumpling was overjoyed.

It puffed with meaning.

It puffed with importance

and yeast.

This time, the ugly dumpling was **NOT** ignored or overlooked.

COCKROACH!

Cockroach?

Cockroach.

The other steamed buns were

horrified.

Appalled.

But then the ugly dumpling did something quite beautiful.

It reached out an arm.
(Or a leg.)

And it led the cockroach out into the world.

The beautiful, **beautiful** world.

Perhaps the ugly dumpling was not like the other steamed buns after all.

And perhaps that was a **good thing.**